My Spectacular Self

Sometimes Cows Wear Polka Dots

A Tolerance Story

by Shoshana Stopek

illustrated by Román Diáz

PICTURE WINDOW BOOKS
a capstone imprint

For Jon, for accepting me just the way I am —S.S.

Published by Picture Window Books, an imprint of Capstone
1710 Roe Crest Drive, North Mankato, Minnesota 56003
capstonepub.com

Library of Congress Cataloging-in-Publication Data
Names: Stopek, Shoshana, author. | Diaz, Román (Illustrator), illustrator.
Title: Sometimes cows wear polka dots : a tolerance story / by Shoshana Stopek ;
illustrated by Román Díaz.
Description: North Mankato, Minnesota : Picture Window Books, an imprint of Capstone, [2022] |
Series: My spectacular self | Audience: Ages 5-7. | Audience: Grades K-1. |
Summary: Millie is different from the other cows on the farm: she wears polka dots instead of
spots and she definitely stands out from the herd; the other cows make fun of her, but Millie does
not care, instead she flaunts her differences—and when the other farm animals respect and imitate
her the other cows wonder if they should be more tolerant of Millie's uniqueness.
Identifiers: LCCN 2021028473 (print) | LCCN 2021028474 (ebook) | ISBN 9781663984906
(hardcover) | ISBN 9781666332568 (paperback) | ISBN 9781666332575 (pdf) | ISBN
9781666332599 (kindle edition) Subjects: LCSH: Difference (Psychology)—Juvenile fiction. |
Toleration—Juvenile fiction. | Cows—Juvenile fiction. | Animals—Juvenile fiction. | Farm
life—Juvenile fiction. | CYAC: Difference (Psychology)—Fiction. | Toleration—Fiction. |
Individuality—Fiction. | Cows—Fiction. | Domestic animals—Fiction. Classification: LCC
PZ7.1.S7557 So 2022 (print) | LCC PZ7.1.S7557 (ebook) | DDC [E]—dc23
LC record available at https://lccn.loc.gov/2021028473
LC ebook record available at https://lccn.loc.gov/2021028474

Special thanks to Amber Chandler for her consulting work.

Designed by Nathan Gassman

Meet Millie

HOBBIES: bedazzling, making milkshakes, helping friends sparkle

FAVORITE BOOKS: *Cow Bling!* and *We All Have Different Mooooves*

FAVORITE FOOD: fresh grass

FUTURE GOALS: to become a fashion designer and to inspire peace for animals around the world

*START AN
ICE CREAM BUSINESS

GOALS FOR
THIS YEAR

*KNIT EACH OF MY FRIENDS
A POLKA-DOT SWEATER

*HOST A TALENT EXTRAVAGANZA

*EXPERIMENT WITH STRIPES

Millie was a VERY unique cow. While the other cows had the usual spots, Millie wore polka dots!

The other cows made milk. Millie made milkshakes.

The other cows meandered and took their time.
Millie SASHAYED and SPRINTED.

Millie didn't mind standing out from the herd. She was PROUD to be herself. But some of the cows felt differently.

They teased her and made her the laughing stock of the herd. And, worst of all, they excluded her.

Millie could have gotten upset. But remember, Millie was a VERY unique cow. So she milked it for all it was worth.

She BEDAZZLED, GLITTERED, and BLINGED out her entire wardrobe.

She SPICED up her shakes with exotic flavors.

And, she added a few more steps to her repertoire: the SAUNTER, the SHIMMY, and the HIPPITY-HOP.

Word spread quickly about Millie around the farm.

And then, the most UNEXPECTED thing happened . . .

Parker Pig revealed that he was secretly a tap dancer.

Rick Rooster broke out in opera tunes.

And wouldn't you know it, Sally Sheep had always wanted to be a hair stylist!

A few of the animals weren't so sure that Millie should trust the cows. But she wasn't worried.

Because as long as she stayed true to herself, ANYTHING was possible.

If everyone accepted each other, they could ALL shine together. And Millie's sparkle would be especially bright.

Practice Tolerance

Tolerance is seeing that your way isn't the only way. Being tolerant means being respectful of the differences among people. It doesn't mean you have to agree with everyone all the time. In fact, you can agree to disagree. Just be open and kind. There are lots of ways to practice tolerance.

Be kind. A classmate is sitting alone at lunch. Invite that person to sit with you.

Be patient. Your friend might take longer to tie her shoe than you do. Wait patiently for her to be done.

Include everyone. Try and play with a new friend at recess or invite someone new over to your place to play.

Accept other people's differences. Your friend celebrates Christmas and you don't. Talk about the different holidays you celebrate.

Be understanding. Everyone looks different and has different family structures and beliefs. You don't have to understand everything about someone else, but you need to respect them.

Tolerance Matters

1. Do you have any personality traits that you think are like Millie?

2. Did you know that herds stay together for protection? They are their own community. Has anyone ever made you feel "outside the herd" because of how you act? How did that feel?

3. Sometimes other people act very differently than we do. It is important to allow them to be a part of the community. To be tolerant or accepting, try to think of things you have in common. What did all the other cows have in common with Millie?

4. Do you know someone who makes you feel brave? What traits does that person have?

5. How can you always make everyone in your community feel free to express themselves?

About the Author

Shoshana Stopek is the author of numerous books for kids and grown-ups. Her picture book series My Spectacular Self includes *Hammock for Two, Out-of-Control Rhino, Heads Up!*, and *Sometimes Cows Wear Polka Dots*. Shoshana grew up in New Jersey, where she learned how to make new friends, fly a kite, and bedazzle a wardrobe. Now she lives in Los Angeles with her husband and daughter where she writes and occasionally still bedazzles. Visit her at shoshanastopek.com.

About the Illustrator

Román Díaz was born in Mexico. Since he was a child, he always wanted to draw like adults. Now that he is an adult he likes to draw like children. He's created illustrations for books, video games, and many other projects. He likes to eat colorful fruits and vegetables and admires animals in documentaries because it seems they have superpowers.